How A SPIDER
Saved Christmas

ISBN 978-1-64670-597-9 (Paperback)
ISBN 978-1-64670-598-6 (Hardcover)
ISBN 978-1-64670-599-3 (Digital)

Covenant Books, Inc.
11661 Hwy 707
Murrells Inlet, SC 29576
www.covenantbooks.com

How A SPIDER
Saved Christmas

SARGIS SARIBEKYAN

With Illustrations by
Gevorg Endza Babakhanyan

Chapter 1

The spider had big, sparkling black eyes with long, gangly, fuzzy legs. This horrible, terrible spider lived in the dark attic, hanging from the ceiling. When night fell, and little Michael went to sleep, this spider would sneak into his bedroom and scare him. Of course, this was only in Michael's imagination as there was no actual spider.

"Sleep tight, little Michael. There is no spider in sight." This was something that his father, mother, and grandmother would tell him often. Even his grandfather, who he trusted most, was unable to convince Michael.

"Spiders are not that scary. They don't want to harm little kids," said Grandpa.

Yet Michael was still afraid.

Today Michael is going to have a sleepover in his grandparent's home but here too, he cannot sleep.

Though Michael is sleepy, his eyes are wide open. He repeats to himself, "When I close my eyes, this horrible, terrible spider will sneak in from the chimney and find me in my bed."

Michael was tossing and turning under his soft blanket. Nothing helped. He hid under his pillow, covering his eyes and ears. Nothing seemed to help. He couldn't sleep.

It was quite late, and only the streetlights peeked through the window. The trees were swaying from side to side, and Michael was gazing at the wall. The shadows from these trees appeared then disappeared.

He saw these shadows coming closer and closer to him. Thinking that this strange, huge, and ugly spider was trying to sneak into his room, quickly, he jumped out of bed and turned on the lamp.

In a flash, the shadow disappeared.

5

To ensure he was safe, he shouted out for his grandpa. Michael's bedroom door quietly opened, and his grandpa appeared.

"Yes, Michael, is something wrong?"

"Everything is wrong. The horrible, terrible spider was here!"

"We already talked about it. Spiders don't want to scare little boys or girls. I am not seeing any spider in your bedroom."

Michael continued, "Grandpa, a horrible, big, sparkling black-eyed spider with long, gangly, fuzzy legs was here to scare me."

To make it even more convincing, Michael took a piece of paper and pencil from his bedside table and drew the spider for his grandpa. "Here is the picture!"

Grandpa lovingly looked at the drawing, then began to laugh and said, "This spider is funny and actually not scary at all. Yet for tonight we shall leave the light on, and tomorrow I will share with you a story."

Chapter 2

Every year over Christmas break, Michael would spend his time with his grandparents and this year would be the same.

These days during the holidays are the best days that he looks forward to every year. There are many gifts, lights, and decorations. The smell of sweets and fresh-baked cookies fills the air. Grandma is the best cook in the entire world, and you should see her kitchen!

Life was almost perfect. Except in the town where his grandparents lived, there was never, ever any snow. Every winter the big trucks would bring snow and drop it into the city park for children to play. That's where Michael would go to build his snowman.

What would Christmas be without snow? thought Michael. *Well, time with Grandpa is most important.*

Today Michael woke up early. He rolled his eyes and smiled. Without the spider in sight, the sun was shining.

Michael exclaimed, "Oh, I almost forgot that today is the day of Christmas Eve, the day I am able to play in the snow."

This was Michael's favorite day of the entire year!

Delicious scents were coming from the kitchen. Grandma was baking her Christmas bread and decorating the yummy cookies with sprinkles.

Out of all the rooms in his grandparents' home, Michael loved the kitchen most.

So to the kitchen Michael ran. "Good morning!" he yelled with a big smile.

"Good morning, kiddo," Grandma said as she kissed Michael's cheeks, which glowed with glee.

Grandpa was already there, sitting with his pot of coffee, reading the newspaper.

Michael reached out to the cookies.

"Go brush your teeth, Michael," Grandma said. "Then go sit with Grandpa, and I will bring your milk and cookies."

After breakfast Michael and his grandpa went to the park to build a snowman.

Chapter 3

In the evening Michael's parents arrived for Christmas dinner. Michael was jumping about and shouting as it was the best day ever!

The dinner table was filled with laughter and joy. The meal that Grandma made was scrumptious. After dessert was served and the table was cleared, Michael's mother played the piano as Grandma sang.

Grandpa then invited everyone to sit by the fireplace as he was preparing to tell them all a story, the same story he mentioned to Michael. Michael climbed into his lap to listen.

"This is a story about a Christmas spider."

When Michael heard this, he placed his hand over Grandpa's mouth and exclaimed, "I don't want to hear stories about spiders! They are all big with sparkling black eyes and long, gangly, fuzzy legs. All spiders are horrible, terrible and live in a dark attic."

"Be patient, Michael, and let me tell the story. For in this Book is a magnificent Christmas story about Jesus. If you promise to listen through to the end, you may open a gift from underneath the tree."

Grandpa picked up the old family Bible. "You all know the Christmas story. There is also some old beautiful legend, which is not in this Book, but a story that was passed down from generation to generation, and now it is time for you to hear it too."

Chapter 4

In the land of Judea where flowers are fragrant, the moon is gigantic, where it is always springtime and the evenings are full of miracles, our Savior Jesus was born.

His mother Mary and His father Joseph had a long journey to reach the town called Bethlehem, but they could not find place to stay, so a stable became the birthplace of baby Jesus.

Mary wrapped this child in swaddling clothes and laid Him down in a manger.

An angel began to sing, "Glory, glory, Lord to you, and peace to all He loves on earth."

In the hills of the mountains, surrounding the town, shepherds were watching their sheep. When they heard the angels sing, they spotted a bright shining star in the sky. They trembled with fright at this sight.

The angel said, "You need not fear. I bring you news of great joy that comes to all people. The Savior is born, Christ the Lord. Don't stand and gaze. A sign I give you to follow, as you shall find a baby King swaddled in cloths, sleeping in a manager."

The shepherds ran to this sight and kneeled before Him with great joy and began to pray and praise the Lord, "A Savior is born, hallelujah!" They rushed to town to share the good news that Christ was born.

The people of Bethlehem happily gave thanks to God for such wonderful news. Even the animals in the stable who hosted the Babe King were happy.

Everyone was overjoyed, except one—the cruel King Herod. He was an angry and jealous man. He commanded his soldiers to go to Bethlehem and find baby Jesus.

Chapter 5

At the same time, in the Far East, three wise men spotted a brilliant star rising in the sky. They rejoiced knowing that the star was a sign that the Savior was born.

They followed the star. And when they arrived in Bethlehem, they presented precious gifts of gold, frankincense, and myrrh to baby Jesus.

"We saw the star of the newborn King and came to worship Him."

Mary was confused. "A King?"

"Yes." And they bowed to baby Jesus. The wise men warned the holy family to escape from this place because the cruel King Herod was looking for Jesus.

Joseph heard what the wise men had said. He took his family and headed to Egypt, where the cruel King Herod would be unable to reach them.

The journey was hard. Mary, the baby Jesus, and even the donkey upon which they rode were all tired. Joseph felt bad for his family and found a cave in which they could rest until morning came.

The soldiers of the angry King Herod were in search of Joseph and his family. The night was breezy and dark. And while the family needed heat, Joseph was afraid to light a fire, in fear of the soldiers finding them.

Baby Jesus was cold and hungry. It was dark, and the wind began to howl as the sound of horses and soldiers approached them. This made baby Jesus cry.

Mary quietly sang a song to calm baby Jesus, but it didn't help. Joseph knelt and began to pray. Before finishing and saying amen, a spider appeared in front of them. No one knew where it came from.

The spider hung from the entrance of the cave and wove a web. All of a sudden the skies opened up and pierced through the darkness. The stars from the sky reflected upon the silky web and lit up brilliantly like the lights on a Christmas tree.

Baby Jesus opened His eyes wide, and His cries were silenced as He saw the web's shining colors of silver and gold.

The voices of a soldier were approaching. Suddenly they stopped, and Mary and Joseph heard one of them in a bold voice saying, "There is no need to search this cave, as there is a spider web here. No one could possibly be in there."

And then the soldiers left.

But the spider didn't go anywhere. It stayed in the cave and made clever tricks that amused baby Jesus for the remainder of the night. The spider hung in the air without care. He danced about, and then he vanished. He reappeared and vanished again as if he was playing peek-a-boo with baby Jesus.

Chapter 6

"Ever since that time," Grandpa said, "many hang tinsel on their Christmas trees. This is a reminder of how a spider saved Christmas."

Michael was silent for a moment. "Grandpa, I didn't know this until now and you know what, Grandpa? I love spiders now. I am no longer scared of them." Michael then turned to his Grandma and asked, "May we hang tinsel on our tree?"

Grandma joyfully replied, "Sure. Let me find the box with the tinsel."

"Now Michael you can open my surprise gift," said Grandpa and handed him the large box.

Michael quickly opened the present from Grandpa, and found a big *not* horrible, *not* terrible, *but* a smiling, friendly spider that Michael could treasure forever.

Michael gave everyone a kiss as it was time for him and his new friend to go to sleep. As he jumped into bed, he hugged his spider and said, "Good night, Spidey, good night and Merry Christmas!"

About the Author

A published author of four preaching volumes and five volumes of children's literature, Sargis Saribeykan was educated in Yerevan, Armenia, where he earned his MA in electronic engineering. After completing the seminary in Jerusalem, he now serves as a parish priest of the Armenian Apostolic Church in Arizona. Sargis is married and a father of two.

CPSIA information can be obtained
at www.ICGtesting.com
Printed in the USA
JSHW020836121120
9459JS00005B/2